This book is for my family: little donkey little caterpillar little chilli little bean

FREE AS A CLOUD

Written by BAI Bing
Illustrated by YU Rong

Singing is what small birds dream of, and singing makes them happy.

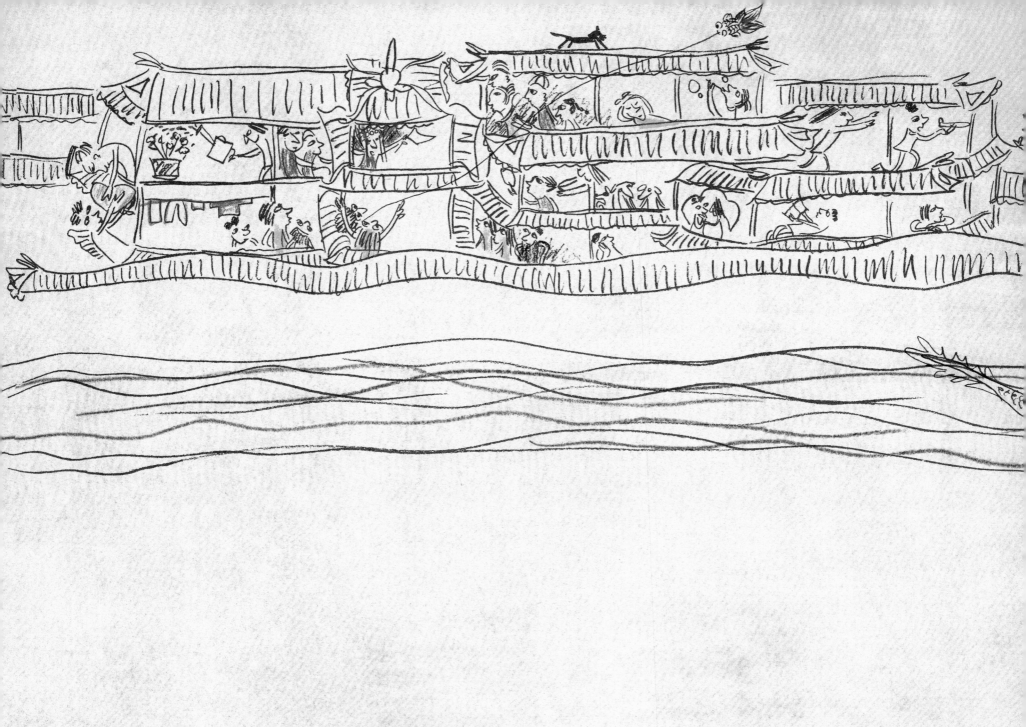

I am a pretty myna.
I am a myna who loves to fly and sing joyfully.

But I see something ahead.
Who are they?
They look happy and friendly.

I don't want to go!
I don't want to leave!

But my new family
loves me so much...

They take me out
for walks.
They give me sweet,
juicy fruit.

But something is
not right. I feel like
something is missing.

My family sees that I am not happy.

"What is it, Sweetie?" they ask. "Are you alright? Would you like a better nest to rest in?"

They buy me the
best cage there is.
It's very pretty and
very spacious.

They give me
nothing but the very
best food.

I can sing.

But I just can't sing
from my heart...

I don't want to be a sad
bird trapped in a cage.

I don't want to sing. I don't want to sing!

My dream is to be free from this cage.

It stops me flying through the forest and up into the clouds.

My family looks at me sadly.
They wonder what I need.

They invite kids to bring their pets for a party.

So many animals come to see me.

I sit quietly as I watch them,
wondering what they could be thinking.
Do they also long to be free?

Then finally, my family understands.
They finally know why I'm always melancholy.
They take me back to the mountains, and...

Wow! It looks like home.
Look at the glorious jungle!
Look at the colourful flowers!

Goodbye, my family.
I will definitely miss you, but I will sing
the sweetest songs for you all.

I'm back, jungle!

I'm back, clouds!

I am so happy I
want to sing out loud.

I want to sing to the other
birds and sing to myself. I am a
beautiful myna as free as a cloud!

www.starfishbaypublishing.com

FREE AS A CLOUD

This edition © Starfish Bay Publishing 2017
First published in 2017
ISBN: 978-1-76036-035-1
Originally published as "Yun Duo Yi Yang De Ba Ge" in Chinese
© Jieli Publishing House Co. Ltd, 2012
Printed and bound in China by Beijing Shangtang Print & Packaging Co., Ltd
11 Tengren Road, Niulanshan Town, Shunyi District, Beijing, China

---

Sincere thanks to Courtney Chow, Marlo Garnsworthy, Lisa Hughes, Christina Phung, Belinda Piscino and Elyse Williams (in alphabetical order) from Starfish Bay Children's Books for editing and/or translating this book.

Starfish Bay Children's Books would also like to thank Elyse Williams for her creative efforts in preparing this edition for publication.